TALES OF WIT
AND WISDOM

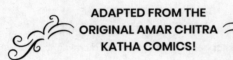

**ADAPTED FROM THE
ORIGINAL AMAR CHITRA
KATHA COMICS!**

First published in India in 2021 by HarperCollins Children's Books

An imprint of HarperCollins *Publishers*

4th Floor, Tower A, Building No. 10, Phase II, DLF Cyber City,

Gurugram, Haryana – 122002

www.harpercollins.co.in

6 8 10 9 7

Text © Amar Chitra Katha 2021

Illustrations © Amar Chitra Katha 2021

P-ISBN: 978-935-422-265-8

E-ISBN: 978-935-422-266-5

Typeset and designed in Patrick hand 22pt/ 27
by Ketan Tondwalkar

Printed and bound at Thomson Press India Ltd

TALES OF WIT AND WISDOM

WRITTEN BY
CHRISTOPHER BARETTO

ILLUSTRATED BY
SHREYA SEN

HarperCollins*Children'sBooks*

AMAR CHITRA KATHA

CONTENTS

THE TEN GREATEST FOOLS

Emperor Akbar enjoyed testing Birbal's intelligence. He would often ask him tricky questions and have the strangest demands. One day, Emperor Akbar summoned Birbal and said, "Birbal, only wise and learned men come to meet the Emperor. For a change, I'd like to meet a fool. Bring me the ten greatest fools in the city! I give you a month's time."

"As you wish, *Jahanpanah*. But, it wouldn't take that long," said Birbal in a mild tone. He then set out to search for the ten greatest fools in the city.

On the way, he came upon an unusual sight. A man was carrying a bundle of sticks on his head while riding a horse. Intrigued, Birbal asked him, "Why carry the bundle on your head instead of placing it behind you, on the saddle?"

To which, the man replied, "*Huzoor,* I really value this horse. After years of serving me, he has become quite old and weak. This bundle of wood might be too heavy for him to handle. So, to relieve him a bit, I'm carrying it for him!"

Upon hearing this absurd reasoning, Birbal thought to himself, "Aha! There's my first fool!"

He then turned to the man and said to him, "Come with me and you will never have to carry another bundle in your life."

And so, having found his first fool, Birbal continued looking for more. Just then, he noticed a man lying flat on his back with his arms in the air. Thinking that the man was sick, Birbal immediately jumped from his horse and rushed towards the man.

As Birbal tried to lift him up, the man exclaimed, "Please don't touch me!"

"Why? Does it hurt? You look like you need medical attention," said Birbal in a concerned tone.

"I'm fine! It's just that my wife has asked me to buy a pot this big," replied the man, "if I move my hands then I won't be able to get the right measurement. I'm

very scared of my wife and if I
get the wrong pot, she will scold me
for the rest of my life! I can't let
that happen."

And just like that, Birbal had found his
second fool.

Birbal told the man that he would buy
him pots of all shapes and sizes as long
as he followed
him. Birbal
picked him up
and they were
on their way
when suddenly...

THUD!

An old man crashed into Birbal! Birbal immediately turned back and shouted, "What is wrong with you? Are you blind?!" The humble old man immediately kneeled down and began apologising. He said to him, "A thousand apologies, *Huzoor*. Actually, I wanted to know how far my voice could go. So, I let out a

HUGE

scream and started running after it. But alas, due to this accident, I will have to start from scratch now."

Birbal couldn't believe it. His third fool had literally fallen into his arms. He told the old man that he would give him two *mohurs** if he followed him and led all three fools to his palace.

Birbal asked the three men to reside at his palace for the time being. He didn't

(*Gold coins of India, introduced by Mughal princes in the 16th century and later used by the British)

have to go too far to find his next set of fools.

At a little distance from his palace, he found two men quarrelling. They were hurling punches at each other.

POW! DISHOOM! SMACK!

Birbal immediately intervened. "Why are you both fighting?" asked Birbal. "*Huzoor*, he threatened to set his tiger on my buffalo!" exclaimed the first man.

Birbal was a bit confused. He didn't see any animals around. He asked the men, "But, I don't see a tiger or a buffalo."

"Oh, you will, *Huzoor*," said the second man, "If God appears before us and grants us a wish each, you will."

The first man grew red with anger and screamed, "Did you hear that, *Huzoor*?! If I ask God for a buffalo, he insists on asking God for a tiger to eat up my wish!"

In that moment, the man exploded and began fighting with the second man again.

Birbal was left speechless. He didn't know what to do. Just then, a voice said, "Only a fool would take these fools seriously!"

Birbal immediately turned and saw a man approaching him with a jar of oil.

The man then said, "If I am wrong then let my bones break to bits and my blood run like this oil." And...

CRAAAAAAAAAASH!

He smashed the jar on the ground.

Immediately, the man regretted his decision. He said, "Ah, what a fool I am to waste such a good jar and such pure oil."

Birbal smiled. It isn't everyday that a fool would call himself one. Without further ado, he took all three men back to his palace and left them with

the other three fools.

Now, Birbal had six fools in total.

After a tiring day of searching for fools, Birbal decided to take a walk at night. The moon was shining bright and it lit up the entire city.

Just then, Birbal came across a
man who was looking for something
on the ground.

"What are you looking for?" Birbal asked
the man.

"I'm looking for my ring, *Huzoor*."

"Did you drop it here?"

"No, I dropped it over there, under
that tree."

"Then why are you
searching for it on the
open ground?"

"Because, *Huzoor*, it's
brighter over here. So,
this is the best place to

look for it."

"And that's seven!" Birbal thought to himself and promised the man that he would buy him a new ring if he followed him. The man agreed without any hesitation.

On their way to the palace, Birbal noticed an old man searching for something near

a sand-pile. Birbal immediately rushed to his aid.

"What seems to be the problem, good man?" asked Birbal.

"Ah, *Huzoor*, perhaps you could help me," said the old man, "I hid my ring in a hole in this sand-pile but now I can't seem to find it. I'm doomed!"

"Why didn't you mark the spot?" asked Birbal.

"I naturally did, *Huzoor*," said the old man, "There was a cloud right above the spot where I hid the ring. But alas, that cloud betrayed me and has now vanished and with it, so has my ring."

Birbal was on a roll! He had found the eighth fool just like that. He took both the men with him to his palace. Soon, he was ready to present all the fools to the Emperor.

The next day, Birbal entered Emperor Akbar's court with all the fools. Emperor Akbar was surprised to see him back already.

"I didn't expect you to return so soon, Birbal," said Emperor Akbar.

"Well, *Jahanpanah*," said Birbal, "everyone knows it's easier to find fools than wise men."

Birbal proceeded to recount his encounters with each and every man to the Emperor. However, Akbar was not pleased.

"Birbal! I asked you to bring me ten fools!"

"That's right."

"These are only eight fools. Where are the remaining two fools?"

"They're right here, *Jahanpanah*."

"Where?"

"Pardon me but that would be the two of us, my king."

"WHAT!"

The entire court fell silent, for no one would ever talk to the Emperor with such disrespect.

"How are you and I fools, Birbal? Explain yourself this instant or be ready to face the consequences," said Akbar in sheer anger.

"Well, you see, *Jahanpanah*, out of all these men, we have been the biggest fools. You for sending me on such an errand and I for obeying you!"

HAHAHAHAHAHAHA!

The entire court, along with Emperor Akbar, burst into laughter. Birbal had once again dazzled the entire court with his sheer wit and humour.

THE MOUSE MERCHANT

One fine day, a young man called
Shantilal was wandering around the busy
streets of Varanasi looking for a job.
While he was walking, he noticed two
men talking. One of them was the royal
treasurer. The other was his friend,

known to be a wise man.

"You are highly valued by the king, my friend," said the royal treasurer. "Thanks to you, the treasury is overflowing with riches. How do you do it?"

"It's simple," said the wise man. "One must have enterprise and initiative."

Intrigued by these words, Shantilal began following the two. The duo then came across a dead mouse. The wise man said, "Now take this dead mouse for example. Even if someone doesn't have money, as long as they have initiative, they can start a business with this dead rodent."

HAHAHAHAHAHAHAHAHAHA!

The royal treasurer burst into laughter.
He could not believe what his friend
had just said. The two of them walked
away. However, what seemed like a joke
to the royal treasurer, really intrigued
Shantilal.

He picked up the dead mouse and thought
to himself, "The treasurer was right
about this being an absurd idea. But, can
I do something with this *dead* mouse?"

As Shantilal walked on holding a dead
mouse by its tail, wondering who would

want to pay money for it, something grazed by him.

MEOOOOOOOOOOOOOOW!

A cat tried to pounce on the dead mouse, dangling from Shantilal's hand, but missed.

"You naughty little cat, come back!" said his master.

As the cat kept jumping, trying to get a hold of the mouse from Shantilal, his master came rushing from behind. "Ah! So this is what made him so restless," said the master. He then turned towards Shantilal and said, "Good sir, will you sell your mouse to me? It will serve as the perfect meal for my little cat here."

Without any hesitation, Shantilal smiled and said, "Why yes, for just one paisa, the mouse is yours!"

The deal was struck and with that one

paisa, Shantilal made his first profit!

Now, all he had to do was figure out what he could do with that one coin. Just then, his eyes settled on some sweet, delicious jaggery at a grocery store. He went to the store and bought a paisa's worth of jaggery.

The next day, he filled a pot with some water and travelled to the outskirts of the city. There, he patiently waited under a tree.

At noon, he saw a couple of flower gatherers travel back to the city from the forest after an entire day of flower picking. They were exhausted and thirsty.

"Brothers and sisters," he said. "You must be tired. Rest under this tree and have some water and jaggery."

Upon hearing these words, the flower-gatherers' faces lit up. They quenched their thirst and ate some jaggery. Pleased by Shantilal's gesture, each of the workers gave him a bunch of flowers in return. As they were leaving, they requested Shantilal to bring water the next day as well. Shantilal was more than happy to fulfill their request.

Now having a bunch of flowers with him, Shantilal headed straight to the temple in the city. There, he sold the same flowers to devotees who had come to worship the lord. He managed to sell all the flowers and earn eight paisas.

With that money, he bought a bigger pot and some jaggery and headed back to the same spot the next day. This time, he offered some more jaggery to the workers. Later, with the leftover water

and jaggery,
Shantilal went a little
further and offered his goods to some
grass-cutters working in the fields.

"Young man, you have been too kind.
Please let us know how we can return the
favour," said one of the workers.

"I don't need anything at present,"

replied Shantilal and went about his way.

A month passed by and things were normal for Shantilal. Until one day...

KRAAA KOOOOOOOOOM!

A huge storm broke out! The wind was so strong, Shantilal could barely keep his balance. After an hour of raging, the storm passed. But, the aftermath of the storm was terrible. The wind had blown down leaves and branches everywhere. Shantilal knew that no one would willingly want to clean up the mess. So he thought to himself, "If there's money in a dead mouse then there's definitely money in leaves and broken branches."

The next morning, Shantilal headed straight to the palace garden and found a worried gardener. He asked him, "Are you facing any problem, sir?"

The worried gardener replied, "Can't you see?! The garden is littered with branches and leaves! What's worse is that the king is expected any moment now. If he sees this mess, he will surely punish me."

Shantilal thought for a moment and said, "Well, I can help you clear these branches as long as I can keep them."

The gardener's frown turned upside down. He immediately agreed.

Shantilal turned around and said, "I'll be back in a while with some help."

He didn't have to go too far. Just near the palace, some children were playing. He got hold of them and offered them some jaggery. The kids were ecstatic with this offer.

Shantilal then asked them, "Would you boys like some more?"

"YES!" they replied in unison.

"Well, you're going to have to earn it then! Come with me to the gardens in the king's palace," said Shantilal.

The kids were ready to work for their jaggery. They readily followed Shantilal to the palace garden.

There, he asked the kids to gather all the branches. The energetic kids managed to pick them up in no time and

received a delicious reward for their efforts.

All the branches and sticks were stacked in a huge pile outside the king's palace gates, and Shantilal stood wondering what to do now. Just then...

SCREEEEEEEEEEEEEEECH!

A bullock cart halted next to him. In the cart, there was a potter who had set his eyes on the branches. "Those branches, are those for sale?"

"Why, yes, of course!" said Shantilal.

As Shantilal was loading the branches onto the cart, the potter thought to himself, "I finally have all the wood I'll need to fire the pots specially ordered by the king."

After a successful deal, Shantilal was wandering around in the marketplace where he overheard two men talking. They were discussing a horse dealer who was rumoured to be visiting the city to sell 500 horses!

Shantilal quickly headed to the fields where his grass-cutter friends were working and said to them, "Friends, remember when I gave you all jaggery a few days ago? I am here to seek a favour in return! I want a bundle of grass from each of you and I want you to promise me that you won't sell any grass until tomorrow afternoon."

The grass-cutters were confused at first but soon agreed to Shantilal's request. Their leader said to him, "There are 500 of

us, so as many bundles will be delivered to your house tonight."

Later that evening, the men delivered 500 bundles of grass.

The next day, the horse trader arrived in the city. He searched far and wide but could not find a single grass seller in all of Varanasi. Finally, he spotted Shantilal's house which had bundles of grass stacked outside. He quickly rushed to the house and offered to buy all the grass for 1000 coins! Shantilal, of course, did not hesitate to make the deal.

A couple of days later, Shantilal got a tip that some merchants were arriving

in Varanasi via boats. He quickly spent some money on good clothes and a chariot and waited at the harbour to receive them at the break of dawn.

When the merchants arrived, Shantilal immediately offered to buy all of their goods. One merchant quoted a price, to which Shantilal agreed. Shantilal

then offered him his ring as security
and set up a camp next to the harbour
and waited.

When the other merchants arrived, they
were shocked to hear that someone had
already bought everything! They knew
that they would have to act quickly
before this new competitor took away all

of their profits.

They immediately went to him and made an offer he simply could not refuse. Shantilal happily accepted the offer and made an enormous profit! All of this from a puny mouse.

Shantilal knew that he had to thank the man who had made all of this possible. He went straight to the wise man and offered him half of his profits.

"Dear sir, please allow me to present these coins to you as my humble *guru-dakshina*," said Shantilal.

"*Guru-dakshina!*" exclaimed the wise man, "But I don't even know you. How could I have taught you anything!"

"Oh, you have taught me a lot," said Shantilal and narrated the entire story to the wise man. The wise man laughed and said, "Well, God helps those who help themselves!"

KESARI'S INVALUABLE TREASURE

Kesari was a humble water-carrier who lived in the city of Varanasi. He was a thin man with strong muscles that could easily carry the weight of two pots of water from the riverbank to the city.

He had a simple job but he did it with complete determination. Despite working hard, he barely made enough money to feed himself twice a day. However, he knew that one day his hard work would pay off.

And it did! A few days later, he made some extra money. He was extremely happy. "*One paisa!* My hard work has finally paid off!" said Kesari to himself.

But this newfound wealth posed a problem. "Now where can I hide this treasure?" he thought. As he was trying to find an answer, he was walking past King Udaya's palace.

King Udaya's palace had a wall so high that no enemy could get past it. Kesari, having some knowledge of architecture, knew that even the best of structures have weaknesses. He began gently tapping on the palace wall. Until...

SKRRRRRRRRRR...

"Aha!" he said to himself, "This brick is loose. I can hide my coin behind this brick. I'll come back for it when the time is right."

And so, Kesari pulled out the brick, placed his treasure inside and put the brick back in its original place. He noted the position of the brick, "My coin is safe under the first brick to the

left of the northern gate, which is the tenth one from the ground. I'm a rich man! Hooray!"

He gleefully went back to his hut.

Kesari worked hard. Every time he would pass the northern gate of the

king's palace, he would look at his treasure and smile, knowing that it was safe there. However, his luck was never good enough for him to ever earn even an extra paisa after that. But that did not bother him.

The years passed and Kesari got married to a beautiful water-carrier.

They built a hut near the southern gate of the city and lived happily.

One day, Kesari's wife wanted to visit the fair in town. However, the couple did not have any extra money to spare. Just then, Kesari said, "Hold on! I have one paisa hidden in a safe place. Let me get that and then we can go and enjoy the fair!"

Kesari's wife jumped in glee. She was extremely delighted. Kesari then sped to retrieve his treasure.

That day, the sun was blazing hot. There was no one to be seen on the streets. Only a hasty Kesari could be seen jolting towards the northern gate of the palace.

King Udaya was resting in his balcony when he saw Kesari run. He thought to himself, "This has to be one of the hottest days of the year and yet this man is running so happily. What secrets does he hold?"

Curious about Kesari's intentions, King Udaya immediately asked for him and had two of his palace guards chase him. The guards were quick to catch hold of him but Kesari was obviously in a hurry. He demanded to be let go of that very instant but the guards refused and dragged him to the king's court.

Soon, Kesari was presented to the king who asked him several questions.

"The earth is scorching hot right now and yet you run as if it's nothing. Don't your feet burn?"

"My desire burns me and not the heat."

"And what would your desire be?"

"My desire is to make my wife happy which will happen once I retrieve my treasure hidden in the northern brick wall of the palace."

King Udaya was pleased with Kesari's determination but he was also curious about the treasure. How much gold could a man be hoarding for him to risk exposing himself to such a dire climate?

"Tell me," said the king, "how much money do you have down there? A hundred gold coins? A thousand? Ten thousand? A lakh?"

As the king increased the amount, Kesari

just shook his head, dismissing every guess. Finally, King Udaya gave up and asked him to reveal the amount.

Kesari responded, "One paisa, Your Majesty."

The entire court burst into laughter.

The king was quite amused to hear this. He immediately gave Kesari one paisa and asked him to go home. Kesari gratefully accepted the coin and said, "Thank you so much, Your Majesty but I will go and get the other coin, too."

King Udaya didn't want the poor man to run all the way to the northern gate so he offered him more money.

"One hundred paisas!"

"One thousand paisas!"

"Ten thousand paisas!"

The king kept raising his offer but humble Kesari was stubborn. Desperate to save Kesari from his misery, the king yelled...

"I WILL GIVE YOU HALF OF MY
KINGDOM AS LONG AS YOU DROP
THE IDEA OF RUNNING FOR THAT
ONE PAISA!"

There was complete silence in
the courtroom.

Kesari thought for a moment and agreed

without any hesitation.

Now a proud owner of half the kingdom, Kesari was asked an important question by the king:

"Which half of the kingdom do you want?"

Kesari thought for a moment and said...

THE NORTHERN HALF!

GOPAL MEASURES THE EARTH

Gopal, a barber residing in Krishnanagar, was well-known for his unfailing humour. He had, on countless occasions, made the king of Krishnanagar laugh in times of distress. He even had free access to

the king's palace! There wasn't a single moment of boredom, thanks to his insightful and witty tales.

One day, the king of Krishnanagar, King Krishna Chandra was sitting on his throne, distressed. Nothing that any of the ministers said cheered him up. There was an air of tension in the courtroom. Just then, Gopal showed up.

One of the courtiers immediately stopped him and said, "The king does

not wish to see you today, Gopal."

At once, Gopal brushed the courtier aside and said, "In that case, I *must* see the king."

He fell at the king's feet and said, "Your

Majesty, I'm here for you."

Meanwhile, the king was in such deep worry that he didn't even look at Gopal's face. He just said to him, "Not today, Gopal. I am worried."

Gopal immediately sprang up and said, "That's not a king's job, Your Majesty!

A king is supposed to pay others to worry on his behalf."

"I suggest you pray to Mother Kali, Your Majesty, just like my friend did earlier today." He then continued to recount his encounter with his friend...

You see, my friend woke up with an

unbearable stomach pain today. So, I asked him if he had tried praying to Mother Kali. He decided to do exactly that. He prayed to Mother Kali to cure him and in return he would sacrifice a buffalo for her.

And in an instant, his stomach ache vanished. He had a big smile on his face. I suggested he rush to arrange for that buffalo that he had promised. My friend burst out laughing and said that a buffalo for Kali would perhaps be too much. She wouldn't be able to do anything with it anyway. He said that he couldn't afford a buffalo either and hoped that Mother Kali would be satisfied with a goat instead.

I didn't know what else to say so I just said that I hoped that Mother Kali would understand and accept a goat as

replacement. But my friend finally did something worse! He went to the temple and said, "Mother, you stay in your temple all day. Maybe you need some exercise. Maybe you should try catching a sparrow on your own."

At that very moment, his pain returned and it was worse than the last time!

My friend understood his mistake and went to Mother Kali and apologised. He even decided to offer her five buffalos and anything else that she desired.

Upon finishing his story, Gopal turned to the king and said, "Now, don't you think that was really clever of Mother Kali?"

The king was hardly amused by the story. Gopal knew that he had to do something about it.

"YOUR MAJESTY! YOUR MAJESTY!" shouted Gopal to try to get the

king's attention.

"WHAT IS IT?!" replied the king with some irritation.

"Why don't you tell me what's bothering you? Maybe I might be able to solve your problem," replied Gopal.

The king knew that even Gopal couldn't solve this problem but he had no other option. So, he confided in him. He said to him, "The Nawab of Murshidabad has ordered someone to measure the length and breadth of THE EARTH!"

Gopal looked at the king as if he was expecting more information. He then said to him, "Oh, is that all? I can accomplish this task for you, Your Majesty."

The king was not amused at the slightest by Gopal's suggestion. He clearly wasn't in the mood for any jokes.

He said to Gopal, "This is an absolutely impossible task to achieve, Gopal.

Moreover, I doubt you will be able to accomplish it. Please do not test my patience during such trying times."

However, Gopal kept on insisting. The king tried to deflect him again by saying, "Gopal, this is not a joke. My very life is at stake here."

"Which is why I want you to trust me and leave this job to me," said Gopal with a smirk on his face.

Seeing Gopal's confidence, the king felt a glimmer of hope. "Maybe Gopal has an answer to my problem after all," the king thought. However, the king still tried to warn Gopal of the consequences.

"This better not be one of your pranks or jokes, Gopal. If you fail, I'll lose my life and you will lose your job."

Gopal shrugged and said, "Neither of which will happen, Your Majesty. All I need is 25 bullock carts and all the silk and cotton thread in town." It was surely an unusual request but the king agreed.

A couple of days later, Gopal was
presented with 25 bullock carts full of
cotton and silk threads. He reached the
Nawab's palace and ordered the bullock
carts to be parked outside. He went
inside and stated the purpose of his

visit. The Nawab was instantly delighted to hear that his curiosity might finally be satisfied.

"All right then," said the Nawab, "where are the measurements?"

Gopal looked at the Nawab, smiled and said, "Follow me, Your Excellency. Your answer is waiting outside for you."

The Nawab followed without any hesitation. Outside, he was surprised to see the row of bullock carts but he kept his patience, curious as the sight was.

"Well, if you take a look at the thread in the first 14 carts, you'll find the length of the Earth. The remaining thread in the 11 carts has the breadth of the Earth," said Gopal with a confident face. Everyone present was a little astounded by his claim, especially the Nawab.

The Nawab held one of the balls of thread and said, "What if the measurement is inaccurate?"

Gopal smirked and said, "In that case,

Your Majesty, you could have it checked or might I suggest you check them personally?"

"Err... I... Uh... It's all right. You may

go now," said the Nawab with visible tension on his face.

"But Your Majesty, don't I deserve a reward for all the trouble I've taken?" asked Gopal.

The Nawab immediately ordered one of his servants to give Gopal 100 gold coins.

When Gopal narrated this incident to King Krishna Chandra, the king started laughing. He said, "I wish I had seen his face!"

"Well, it wasn't exactly a pretty sight, Your Majesty," said Gopal, laughing.

THE BEARER OF MISFORTUNE

Work at Emperor Akbar's palace began quite early in the morning. All the servants would wake up bright and early to make sure that the palace was spick and span, squeaky clean before the Emperor woke up.

One of the workers at the palace was despised and looked down upon by the others. His name was Gulshan. He was a middle-aged man who was known to be the bearer of bad luck. Anyone who saw his face in the morning was convinced that they would have a terrible day.

Word about Gulshan's unlucky nature had spread far and wide. Even the

Emperor had heard murmurs. All the workers tried to avoid him as much as possible. But, Gulshan didn't care. He would mind his business at all times.

One day, Emperor Akbar woke up earlier than usual. He shouted, "Is someone there?! I need my slippers!" The Emperor's words fell on only one pair of ears and they happened to be Gulshan's.

For Gulshan was the only one around at that early hour. He said to himself, "I don't want to be the first person that

the Emperor sees in the morning but on the other hand, he needs assistance. Maybe I can redeem myself."

He reluctantly went into the Emperor's
chambers and helped Akbar.

When Akbar saw Gulshan, he
immediately identified him as the
unlucky man and asked him to send in

other servants.

Sometime later, one of Akbar's servants came running to him and said, "*Jahanpanah*, Prince Khurram is very ill and has been crying for you." Akbar instantly rushed to the child's side and spent several hours with him until the fever subsided.

But it wasn't the end of Emperor Akbar's troubles. He was about to go and have a late breakfast when one of his servants rushed to him and said, "*Jahanpanah*! The Burmese Ambassador has been awaiting an audience all morning."

Emperor Akbar sighed and said, "I'll be right there."

After spending some time with the Burmese Ambassador, the Emperor finally bid him farewell. But at that very moment, one of his ministers reported a rebellion taking place in a remote part of the vast kingdom.

"What! A rebellion?! We must act immediately!"

The Emperor decided to look into the matter personally.

He consulted his clever ministers and commanders. They finally managed to disperse the rebellion. At the end of it, Akbar was extremely tired.

"This has been a really difficult day. To top it all, I haven't even had anything to eat all day."

The servants scurried to get the Emperor a meal. As the Emperor sat down to take a bite, he doubled down and screamed in pain.

AAAAAAAAAAAAAAAAAAAAAAAAH!

The Emperor felt an excruciating pain in his stomach. He called for his physician immediately.

The physician arrived and examined Akbar. After a thorough examination, he advised the king not to eat anything. Emperor Akbar agreed and decided to call it a day.

When he was in bed, his idle thoughts decided to cloud his judgement. He began thinking, "Could it be possible

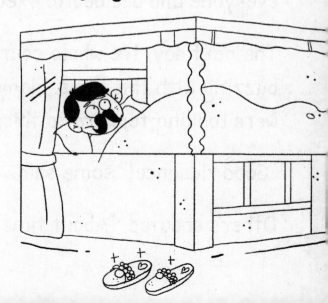

that everything that happened today was because I saw Gulshan's face in the morning? It has to be! He is known to bring bad luck to anyone who sees his face first thing in the morning."

While Akbar was thinking, he was also being tormented by pain, fatigue and most importantly, hunger. Due to this, he made an irrational decision. He concluded that Gulshan was a threat to everyone and decided to execute him.

The next day, the whole court was buzzing with this news. Many people were looking forward to this execution.

"Good riddance!" some said.

Others shouted, "About time!"

While everyone was rejoicing, Birbal
stood in the corner, gloomily. He
knew that the decision was not only
unethical, but also incorrect. Birbal
took it upon himself to defend and
save Gulshan.

He went to Akbar and said to him, "*Jahanpanah*, I would like to ask Gulshan a few questions, if you don't mind?"

Akbar agreed and Gulshan was called in. Birbal began questioning him.

"So, tell me, Gulshan, whom did you meet yesterday when you started your daily chores in the morning?"

"I met nobody, *Huzoor*. There was no one around."

"Then whose face did you first see that morning?"

"I saw Emperor Akbar, *Huzoor*."

Birbal then turned to Akbar and said to

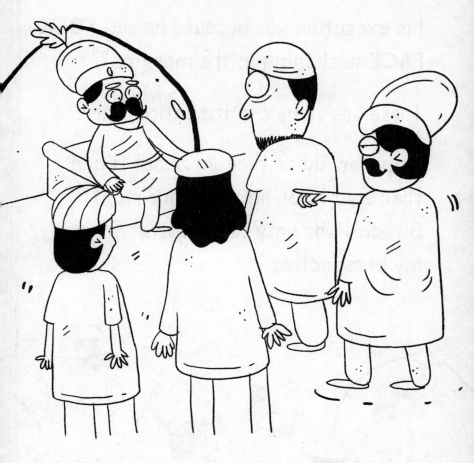

him, "*Jahanpanah*, you claim that the sight of this man was the reason for all your troubles yesterday. But what if he were to claim that the cause of his execution was because he saw **YOUR FACE** first thing in the morning?"

There was silence in the entire court.

Emperor Akbar thought about it and then said to Birbal, "You are right, Birbal. I was only looking at it from my perspective."

He then immediately asked for Gulshan to be released.

Emperor Akbar then said, "Oh Birbal, once again you have saved me from making a rash decision. How can I ever repay you?"

Birbal smiled and replied, "Well, Your Majesty, you can start by being well-fed all day, please!"

GOPAL AND THE HILSA-FISH

It was Hilsa-fish season in Krishnanagar. Everyone wanted a piece of the most precious of fish. The marketplace was full of it, fishermen's nets wouldn't catch anything other than this fish. It was the talk of the town. Even some of the courtiers in King Krishna Chandra's

palace couldn't resist talking about it.

One of the courtiers said, "Your Majesty, you won't believe the size of this Hilsa I caught. It was..."

The king had had enough of it. He grew tired of hearing about the fish.

He said, "STOP IT! I've had it! Why are you talking so much about a fish? Are you a courtier or a fisherman? You are all ministers of the king. I will not have you

talk about fish any longer!"

There was a blanket of silence in the court. You could hear a pin drop.

However, the king soon realised that he had overreacted. He said, "I'm sorry. I should've known that it's Hilsa season and no one, not even Gopal, can stop anyone from talking about it."

Just then Gopal walked in and said, "Did I hear you pose a challenge for me, Your Majesty?"

"Like I said, you can't stop anyone from talking about Hilsa, Gopal."

"Oh, I'm sure I can."

"Is that so? Then let me see you buy a gigantic Hilsa and bring it all the way

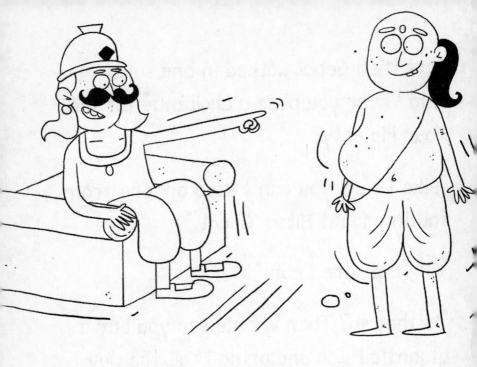

from the market to the palace without anyone asking you about it."

"Challenge accepted, Your Majesty."

And just like that, Gopal pranced out of the palace.

A few days later, early one morning, Gopal's wife got the shock of her life

when she saw him getting ready to go
out. Gopal had shaved only half of his
face, he had covered his face in ash
and had worn clothes that were torn
all over.

She said to him, "Gopal! Why are
you dressed up like this? What's the
meaning of all this?"

Gopal smiled and said, "Oh dear, I'm just going to buy some Hilsa."

Gopal's wife grew worried. She knew he couldn't go out like this. People would never stop laughing at him. She tried to make him stop. She even offered to go and buy some fish on his behalf but he refused. And Gopal insisted on going

out exactly as he was dressed. Gopal's wife feared that perhaps her husband had finally gone crazy.

Gopal bought the Hilsa and began walking from the marketplace towards King Krishna Chandra's palace. There wasn't a single eye in Krishnanagar that didn't look at Gopal and wonder.

Some people laughed while some were concerned. Most importantly, nobody recognised that it was Gopal. They said all sorts of things.

"Look at that comical man!"

"He must be a mystic."

"I think he's definitely a madman."

"What a strange man."

"It's best to keep away from such a clown."

Gopal paid no attention to any of these comments and went about his way. He finally reached the palace gates where he was stopped by the guards.

"Halt at once!" they said, "What do you want?"

Gopal replied, "I wish to see the king."

The guards then began mocking him and told him that under no circumstances could a man dressed like him meet the king. But Gopal wasn't going to give up so easily. He had an idea.

Soon, Gopal began singing loudly. He wasn't the most melodious man in Krishnanagar. To top it all, he even began dancing wildly. Soon a crowd gathered all around him. The guards were slowly losing their patience.

"Let me in," said Gopal, while dancing around frantically.

"No way," replied the

guards. The guards and Gopal kept going back and forth.

The king soon heard this commotion and ordered one of the guards to present the man in front of him at once. When Gopal came to the court, one of the courtiers immediately recognised him and said, "Wait! That is Gopal!" At that moment, all the guards let go of him and the entire court was in shock.

The courtiers started whispering amongst themselves.

"See, I told you! Gopal would lose his mind one day!"

"Is this the man who speaks to the king so often?"

"You know, Gopal. This must be some sort of practical joke."

However, not one courtier could pinpoint the real reason as to why Gopal would appear thus. Why would someone put himself through such humiliation?

The king then intervened and said, "Gopal, what is the meaning of this? Why have you come to the palace dressed like this? Is this another one of your jokes?"

Gopal smiled and replied, "Your Majesty, you seem to have forgotten something.

Strangely enough, no one seemed to be interested in this Hilsa today. Everyone just wanted to know the reason behind my current state. Not one soul asked me about the fish. Not. One. Soul."

That's when King Krishna Chandra and the other courtiers remembered the challenge he had thrown at Gopal. They all burst into laughter.

King Krishna Chandra turned to Gopal, "Well done, Gopal. Once again, you have achieved the impossible!"

THE MATCHLESS WIT

Tenali Raman was a poet-jester in the court of Krishnadeva Raya, the great king of Vijayanagara. He was perhaps the smartest man in the room. His quick thinking and wit not only saved lives but often entertained the king and courtiers as well.

One day, a scholar from Varanasi
visited Krishnadeva Raya's palace. He
challenged the scholars at his court to
a debate on any topic they liked. The
king accepted this challenge. However,

the king's learned court scholar, Panditaraj, knew that he didn't stand a chance against this man and told the king as much.

Just then, Tenali Raman interrupted the king and said, "Your Majesty, I'll do it."

King Krishnadeva Raya was a little unsure as wit isn't the same as scholarship. However, Raman's reassuring words convinced him.

That evening, everything was set in the court. Tenali Raman arrived with a bunch of disciples and a large bundle of manuscripts wrapped in cloth. Once he was seated, the learned scholar asked him, "So, which work have you chosen to debate on?"

Tenali Raman replied, "Let's start with an easy one. I suppose you're familiar with *Tilakashtha Mahisha Bandhana of...*"

"WHAT?! Tilakashtha..."

The renowned scholar's face froze, for he knew nothing of the subject Tenali Raman was challenging him with.

He said to him, "I beg your pardon, O learned one, but I do not know of this that you speak of."

The entire court was in shock. Tenali then said, "That's odd, since even cowherds in our city are familiar with this."

The learned scholar was in shock. How could he, who had studied about everything in great detail, not know of something that a mere cowherd knew? The scholar stood up, humbly bowed down to Tenali Raman, accepted his defeat and left the court.

Once he had left, the King thanked Raman for saving the kingdom's reputation. Panditraj asked Raman about the topic he had spoken of. Raman smiled and unpacked the bundle to reveal bundles of stalks. He said, "Behold! Tilakashthas - the stalks of the sesame plant that have been tied

together with the *Mahisha Bandhana* - the rope with which buffaloes are tethered."

HAHAHAHAHAHAHAHAHAHAHAHA!

The entire court erupted into laughter. Everyone laughed, except Panditraj. He couldn't accept the fact that he had been deceived by Raman. He decided that he

would have his revenge.

Panditraj told the king, "But Maharaj, he has insulted a learned man. He must be punished!"

The king agreed and asked Panditraj how Raman should be punished, to which he replied saying, "Off with his head!"

King Krishnadeva Raya trusted Tenali Raman to take care of himself so he

decided to humour Panditraj. He
called his guards and ordered them to
take Raman to the banks of Tungabhadra
and cut off his head with one sweep of
their swords.

The guards got hold of Tenali Raman and
told him about the King's orders. Tenali
Raman smiled and said, "Well, if that's
what the king wants then I shall accept
my fate."

On the banks of Tungabhadra, the guards asked Tenali Raman for his last wish.

He said, "I want both of you to cut off my neck the moment I call out to Mother Kali. I must die with Mother Kali's name on my lips." The guards found it a bit odd but they agreed to his final wish.

So, Tenali Raman began praying and then he said...

JAI MAA KALI!

At that moment both the guards swung their swords and just like that, Tenali Raman was gone. One of the guards said, "Huh? Where's his body?"

"It's right here!" said Tenali after popping his head out of the water with a smile on his face. He had dodged their blow by simply ducking.

The guards got furious and said, "STAND UP! We will make sure we get you this time."

"Uh-uh-uh," said Tenali Raman, "The king had said *cut off his head with one sweep of your sword.* You're going to

have to ask for his permission for the second one."

The guards took him to the king and narrated the entire incident. Panditraj got furious and said, "Your Majesty, I suggest you bury him up to his neck and let him be trampled to death by an elephant." The king agreed and ordered his guards to do the same. But he feared that Tenali might not get out of this.

The guards did exactly as they were instructed to. They took Tenali to a patch of land far away, dug a pit, put him inside and sealed the pit up to his neck. They then decided to come back with elephants after lunch, leaving Tenali Raman completely...

...unattended.

A washerman carrying a huge bundle of clothes

was passing by. He saw Tenali Raman and assumed that he was a very learned yogi who had found a new way to meditate. He went to seek his blessings.

As soon as he saw the man approach, Tenali figured that this was his ticket out of the pit. As the washerman lowered his head and asked for blessings, Tenali said, "Who am I to bless you, brother? I'm just a humble washerman like you." The washerman was puzzled.

Tenali continued, "The reason I am in this pit is because it is treating my hunchback. Being buried like

this for an hour will heal me, I have been told."

The washerman didn't believe Tenali. So, Tenali asked him to dig him out of the pit to see for himself. When Tenali came out of the pit with an erect back, the washerman couldn't believe his eyes. He insisted on trying it as well. And so, the washerman got into the pit that had been created for Tenali Raman. In return, Tenali agreed to deliver the clothes the washerman was carrying, which incidentally needed to be delivered to King Krishnadeva Raya's palace.

The guards went back to the place with an elephant only to find the washerman crying for help. When the king found out about this, he laughed and said, "Oh Tenali, I doubt anyone can match your wit!"

ABOUT BIRBAL

Born Mahesh Das, Birbal was the main advisor and commander in Emperor Akbar's court. Birbal was famous for his intelligence and wit and has been a central character in several folktales from the Mughal period.

People often came to Emperor Akbar's court with tricky problems which only Birbal could solve. Emperor Akbar also enjoyed challenging Birbal. To everyone's surprise, Birbal was always a step ahead. He had an answer to every question and a solution to every problem.

Birbal used common sense and mixed it with humour, leading to solutions that not only had a lesson, but also left the Emperor and his court amused.

To this day, the tales of Akbar and Birbal are loved by children and adults alike.

ABOUT TENALI RAMAN

Tenali Ramakrishna, or Tenali Raman as he is more popularly known, was a renowned poet, scholar and thinker of the 16th century. However, he was best known as the special advisor of Krishnadeva Raya, King of the Vijayanagara Empire, in present-day Andhra Pradesh.

King Krishnadeva Raya was the third ruler of the Tuluva dynasty. He is considered to be its greatest ruler. He went by several titles, some of which are 'Lord of the Kannada Empire', 'Andhra Scholar King' and 'King of Three Kings'.

The legacy of King Krishnadeva Raya lives on in the great Kannada and Telugu literature composed under his patronage. The stories of Tenali Raman are also popular all over the world.

ABOUT GOPAL

Coming from humble origins, Gopal Bhand was a barber in Bengal, who also happened to be one of the most trusted confidantes of King Krishna Chandra Roy.

King Krishna Chandra Roy ruled large parts of Bengal between 1728 and 1782 from his seat in Krishnanagar. This was a time of change in India, particularly in Bengal. Mughal rule was giving way to the British in large parts of the country. King Krishna Chandra Roy played a pivotal role in the politics of the time. One of his notable rivals was the Governor of Murshidabad, who was mostly referred to as 'Nawab'.

Fans of witty stories from India's folklore are familiar with Tenali Raman and Birbal. However, Gopal Bhand, too, had his fair share of credit for solving the king's problems with his wit and wisdom.

The stories in this collection are adapted from the following ACK original comics.

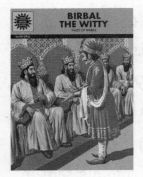

Birbal the Witty

'The Ten Greatest Fools' has been adapted from the comic book, *Birbal the Witty*, written by Kamal Chandrakant, illustrated by Ram Waerkar and edited by Uncle Pai. The book was released in 1978.

The Mouse Merchant

The stories 'The Mouse Merchant' and 'Kesari's Invaluable Treasure' were adapted from the Amar Chitra Katha comic of the same name, that was released in 1982. The book was a collection of stories from the Jataka Tales. It was illustrated by Chandrakant D Rane, written by Subba Rao and edited by Uncle Pai.

Gopal the Jester

The stories 'Gopal Measures the Earth' and 'Gopal and the Hilsa-fish' are adapted from the Amar Chitra Katha comic Gopal the Jester. It was released in 1981 and adapted from the Bengali stories by Urmila Sinha. It was illustrated by Souren Roy and edited by Uncle Pai.

Birbal the Clever

'The Bearer of Misfortune' is adapted from the story 'The Man Who Brought Ill Luck', which appeared in the short comic collection, *Birbal the Clever*. It was released in 1980, and was written by Meera Ugra. The collection was edited by Uncle Pai and illustrated by Ram Waerkar.

Raman the Matchless Wit

'Tenali Raman the Matchless Wit' has been adapted from the short story appearing in the comic, *Raman the Matchless Wit*, originally published in 1980. It was edited by Uncle Pai, written by Subba Rao and illustrated by Ram Waerkar.

About ACK

Amar Chitra Katha was founded in 1967 and is a household name in India. It is synonymous with the visual reinvention of the quintessentially Indian stories from the great epics, mythology, history, literature, oral folktales and many other sources.

With a heavy bent on authenticity and meticulous research, Amar Chitra Katha prides itself on being the most informative and trusted storyteller for children. The stories in this series have been adapted directly from the comics for young readers.

Today, Amar Chitra Katha is a cultural phenomenon, custodian of more than 400 comics in 20+ languages that have sold 100+ million copies to date. Amar Chitra Katha is available in bookstores, online and across digital platforms.

AMAR CHITRA KATHA FOLKTALES SERIES

India's rich tapestry is woven together
by her stories. These tales can be from
the great epics and mythology, or from the
ancient history of this rich land. But sometimes
the stories of the people, passed down from
generation to generation — told at bedtimes
and celebrations, in schools and homes —
are the most astounding. These are the
folktales that are part of the great collective
inheritance from our past generations.

This series brings together some of the
greatest folktales in the Amar Chitra Katha
catalogue. Each book in the series is adapted
from the original Amar Chitra Katha comics
and aims to bring the reader closer to the
thoughts and traditions that make up
our country's identity.